CAVE EXPLORER

WILD JOBS

LAURA K. MURRAY

CREATIVE EDUCATION · CREATIVE PAPERBACKS

PUBLISHED BY CREATIVE EDUCATION AND CREATIVE PAPERBACKS
P.O. Box 227, Mankato, Minnesota 56002
Creative Education and Creative Paperbacks are
imprints of The Creative Company
www.thecreativecompany.us

DESIGN AND PRODUCTION by Joe Kahnke
Art direction by Rita Marshall
Printed in the United States of America

PHOTOGRAPHS by Alamy (13UG 13th, Aurora Photos, Clint Farlinger,
Chris Howes/Wild Places Photography, Marc Muench, David Nixon,
Paulo Oliveira, Really Easy Star/Toni Spagone), iStockphoto (benjaminjk,
BudiNarendra, ramilyan, tbradford), LostandTaken.com, National
Geographic Creative (STEPHEN ALVAREZ, CARSTEN PETER/
SPELEORESEARCH & FILMS), Shutterstock (All-stock-photos, Dmytro
Gilitukha, Husjak, Betti Luna, matkovci, Nik Merkulov, Miloje, pun483,
salajean, Dray van Beeck)

Library of Congress Cataloging-in-Publication Data
Names: Murray, Laura K., author.
Title: Cave explorer / Laura K. Murray.
Series: Wild Jobs.
Includes bibliographical references and index.
Summary: A brief exploration of what cave explorers do on the job,
including the equipment they use and the training they need, plus real-life
instances of exploring caves such as Kentucky's Mammoth Cave.
Identifiers: ISBN 978-1-60818-923-6 (hardcover) / ISBN 978-1-62832-
539-3 (pbk) / ISBN 978-1-56660-975-3 (eBook)
This title has been submitted for CIP processing under LCCN 2017940120.

CCSS: RI.1.1, 2, 3, 4, 5, 6, 7; RI.2.1, 2, 4, 5, 6; RI.3.1, 2, 5, 7; RF.1.1, 3, 4; RF.2.3, 4

FIRST EDITION HC 9 8 7 6 5 4 3 2 1
FIRST EDITION PBK 9 8 7 6 5 4 3 2 1

CONTENTS

YOU ARE DEEP UNDERGROUND.

You carefully squeeze through a narrow passage. Then you enter a giant cavern. Your footsteps echo in the damp, dark cave. Its ceiling is hundreds of feet high!

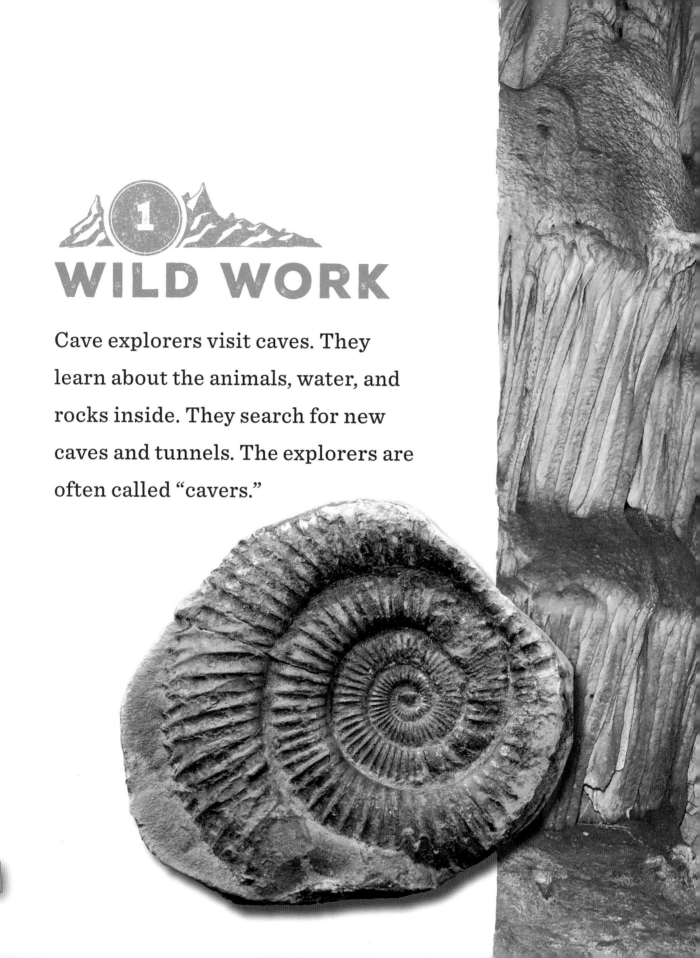

1
WILD WORK

Cave explorers visit caves. They learn about the animals, water, and rocks inside. They search for new caves and tunnels. The explorers are often called "cavers."

Cavers may **SURVEY** the caves to make maps. They take photos and videos. Speleologists (*spee-lee-AH-lo-jists*) are scientists who study caves.

UNDERGROUND PITFALLS

Caves can be long or short. They may have lakes, pits, or waterfalls. Cavers hike, crawl, and climb. They risk falling, drowning, and getting lost or trapped. Cave divers explore underwater caves.

STALACTITES

STALAGMITES

Caves have formations such as **STALACTITES** and **STALAGMITES**. Caves are also home to bats, insects, spiders, fish, salamanders, and other living things. Cavers respect caves and their creatures.

BATS

3
STUDIES IN PROTECTION

Cavers never explore alone. Some cavers study subjects such as **GEOLOGY** or **BIOLOGY**. They might get trained in cave rescue. Cave divers need special water training.

Cavers wear helmets, gloves, and boots. They may wear pads on their knees and elbows. They carry water, food, and a first-aid kit. Each person needs at least three sources of light. They use ropes or ladders for **VERTICAL CAVING**.

KENTUCKY CAVERN

Mammoth Cave is in Kentucky. It is the longest cave system in the world. People have mapped more than 400 miles (644 km) so far.

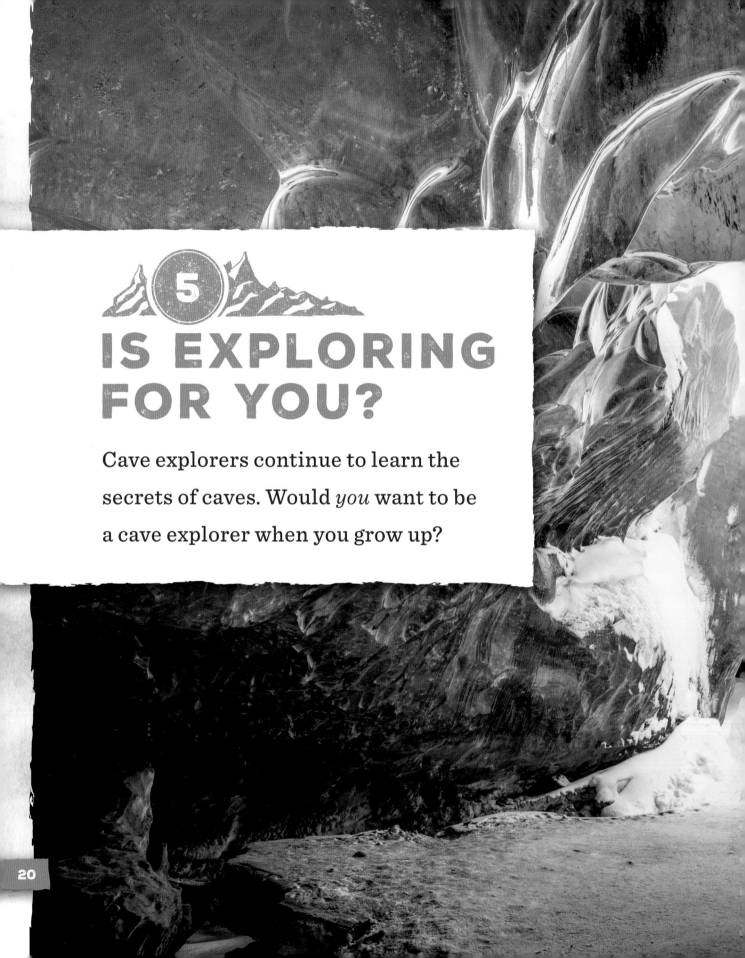

5 IS EXPLORING FOR YOU?

Cave explorers continue to learn the secrets of caves. Would *you* want to be a cave explorer when you grow up?

YOU BE THE CAVE EXPLORER!

Imagine you are a cave explorer. Read the questions below about your wild job. Then write your answers on a separate sheet of paper. Draw a picture of yourself as a cave explorer!

My name is _____. I am a cave explorer.

1. What creatures do you see inside a cave?
2. Is caving scary? Why or why not?
3. What does it sound like inside a cave?
4. What equipment do you bring?
5. What else do you want to learn about caves?

GLOSSARY

BIOLOGY: the science of living things

GEOLOGY: the science of earth and rocks

STALACTITES: rock formations that hang from a cave ceiling

STALAGMITES: rock formations that build upward from a cave floor

SURVEY: to examine an area and record its features

VERTICAL CAVING: a type of cave exploration that requires ropes for large drops and pits

READ MORE

Green, Emily K. *Caves*. Minneapolis: Bellwether Media, 2007.

Loh-Hagan, Virginia. *Extreme Cave Diving*. Ann Arbor, Mich.: Cherry Lake, 2016.

WEBSITES

Dragonfly TV: Caves
http://pbskids.org/dragonflytv/show/caves.html
Watch kids explore a California cave.

Mammoth Cave
https://www.nps.gov/maca/index.htm
Learn more about Mammoth Cave National Park in Kentucky.

Note: Every effort has been made to ensure that the websites listed above are suitable for children, that they have educational value, and that they contain no inappropriate material. However, because of the nature of the Internet, it is impossible to guarantee that these sites will remain active indefinitely or that their contents will not be altered.

INDEX